MOMENTS IN
SPACE & TIME

ROUGH WRITERS ANTHOLOGY

2019

MOMENTS IN
SPACE & TIME

SYMPOSIARCH
PUBLISHING

AN IMPRINT OF MARILEE PUBLISHING, LLC

Editor – Cynthia Gellis
Assistant Editors – Kathy Garr, Faith Pinho
Cover and Book Design – Benjamin Horak
Writing Prompt – Starr Canon
Publishing Production – David Kitchen, Michael Lattimore

Printed in the United States of America

First Printing, 2019 ISBN: 978-1-7322482-4-3 (Paperback)

Library of Congress Control Number: 2019953719

SYMPOSIARCH PUBLISHING
an imprint of MariLee Publishing
P.O. Box 238 Altadena, CA 91003
marileepublishing.com
info@marilleepublishing.com

Rough Writers Toastmasters Club
roughwriters.toastmastersclubs.org

Ordering Information: Special discounts may be available for volume purchases by schools, corporations, associations, and others. To place orders, call (562) 548-2284 or send request to info@marileepublishing.com or contact the publisher at the address above.

First Edition

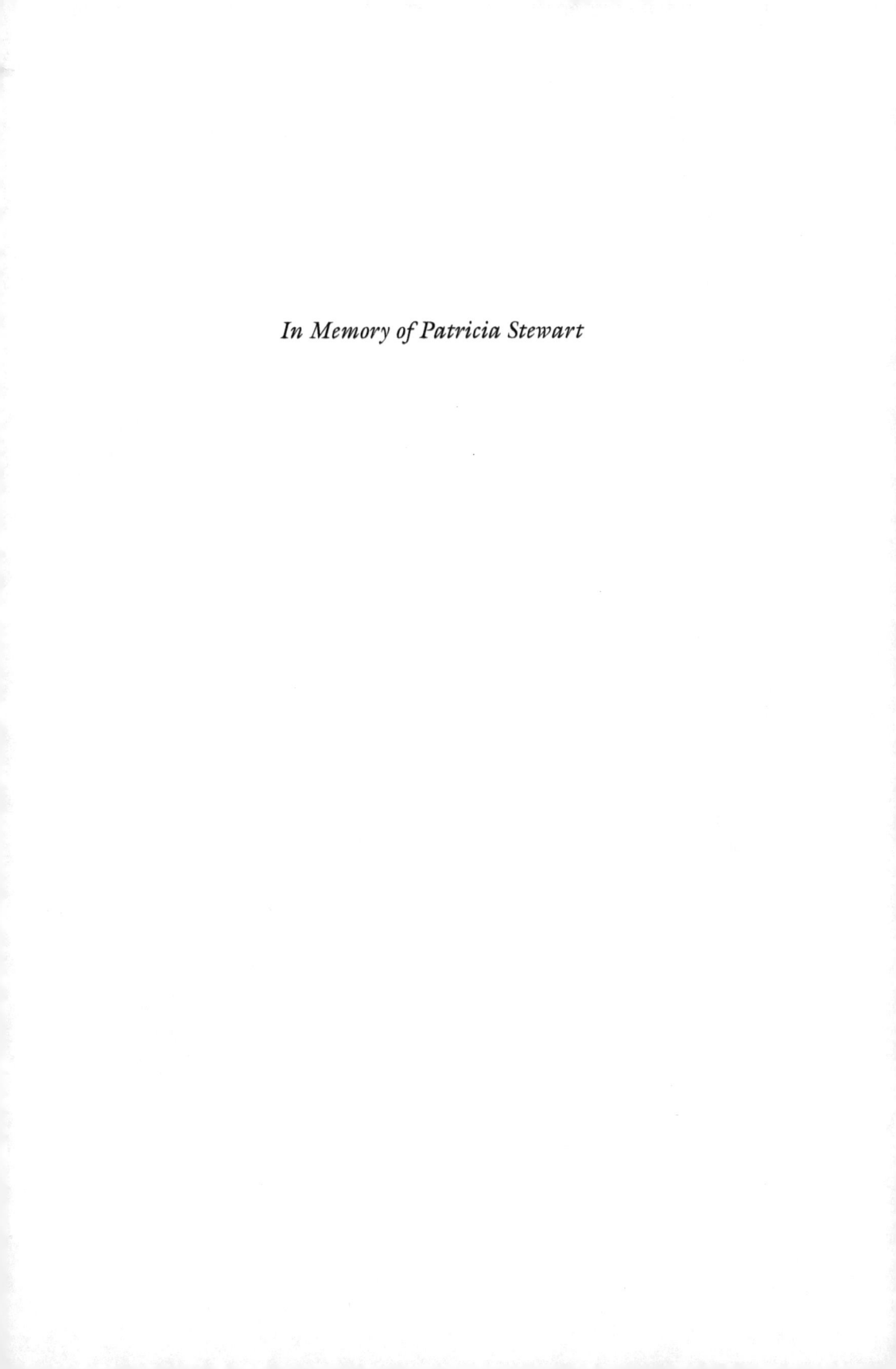

In Memory of Patricia Stewart

Table of Contents

The Rough Writers

A few years ago, several members of Toastmasters International who were aspiring writers had an epiphany: while Toastmasters clubs focus on public speaking, the speeches and feedback that are integral to the Toastmasters curriculum can also be tools for writers. Why not create a hybrid club where experienced public speakers can hone their craft as writers? And where writers can develop their public speaking skills?

With that in mind, the group began meeting on Monday evenings. Word got out, more people joined, and the Rough Writers club was officially founded on March 31, 2015.

The club's name is an homage to the U.S. volunteer cavalry first regiment of the Spanish-American War, a colorful group of characters known as the Rough Riders. Cowboys, prospectors, hunters, gamblers, and Native Americans served on equal footing with Ivy League graduates, polo players, tennis champions, and yachtsmen. The Rough Riders, led by Theodore Roosevelt, were the only cavalry regiment to see battle in that conflict.

The Rough Writers is a similarly colorful group, with diverse characters of all ages and from all walks of life. The group includes distinguished Toastmasters and beginning orators, published authors and novice writers, retired professionals, college students, businesspeople, and educators. However rough their skills may be, members are able to refine and polish their writing and speaking in a supportive and collegial environment.

The Rough Writers meets on Mondays at 7 p.m. in the community room of Fire Station #8, 5373 East 2nd Street, Long Beach, California.

Foreword

Rough Writers is a Toastmasters club that empowers speakers to translate their speeches into prose, and writers to transform their prose into spoken words. We have adapted the Toastmaster program to give writers, new and experienced, a space to grow their communication and leadership skills and hone their craft. This book is a result of our collaborative work.

The writers of this book all started with the same prompt, a picture. Starr Canon has graciously given us permission to reproduce her photograph in this volume. It and information about the artist can be found on page 71.

The diversity of the stories included in these pages reflects the diversity of our club. Even though we come from a wide array of backgrounds, from experienced Toastmasters to new public speakers, from retired professionals to college students, from published authors to novice writers, we all have found something in the image that inspired us to tell a story. I think that you will find the diversity of interpretations as delightful as I have.

As the President of Rough Writers Toastmasters, I am excited to share the many talents of our members as they continue to hone their craft and chase their dreams.

This book is dedicated to the memory of Patricia Stewart, a charter member and editor for the Rough Writers Toastmasters club. Patricia was the editor of our first publication, *Speeches to Books*, and was integral to bringing that project to fruition. She would have been so excited to be part of Rough Writers's second book.

Lydia Martinez,
Distinguished Toastmaster (DTM) • *President, Rough Writers*

Listed are the contributors to the book

Susan Cameron .... *Author*

Cynthia Gellis .... *Author, Editor*

Terrell Harrison .... *Author*

Benjamin Horak .... *Author, Cover and Book Design*

Christopher Gildemeister .... *Author*

Cary Kellems .... *Author*

James Kinstle .... *Author*

David Kitchen .... *Author, Prepared for Publishing*

Lola! Love .... *Author*

Lydia Martinez .... *Author*

Rick Shigio .... *Author*

Carma Spence .... *Author*

Anna Ziss .... *Author*

Michael Lattimore .... *Prepared for Publishing*

Faith Pinho .... *Asst. Editor*

Kathy Garr .... *Asst. Editor*

Starr Canon .... *Photographer*

Acknowledgments

On behalf of the Rough Writers, I would like to thank our intrepid members for making the idea of this book into a reality.

To all of the members who contributed their stories, Susan Cameron, Cynthia Gellis, Terrell Harrison, Benjamin Horak, Christopher Gildemeister, Cary Kellems, James Kinstle, David Kitchen, Lola! Love, Lydia Martinez, Rick Shigio, Carma Spence, and Anna Ziss, thank you for enthusiastically embracing the challenge presented. The diversity of perspectives represented in this volume is a testament to creativity.

To our officers, Susan Cameron, Antionette Emery, Kathy Garr, Torrie Kinley, Lydia Martinez, Rick Shigio, and Patrick Verebely, thank you for your efforts to produce such edifying weekly meetings and for all of the time that you dedicate outside of our meetings to keep this club functioning smoothly.

I would specifically like to mention some of the members who were instrumental in making this book happen: Susan Cameron for masterminding the entire project; David Kitchen and MariLee Publishing for generously assisting us in setting up our imprint, Symposiarch Publishing; Benjamin Horak for contributing his talents as a graphic designer to create our stunning cover and beautiful layout; and Faith Pinho and Kathy Garr for their meticulous proofreading.

Finally, a special thank you to our intrepid leader, Lydia Martinez, without whose knowledge, patience, and equanimity, none of this would have been possible.

It was a pleasure to have the opportunity to take on such an active role in the production of this volume. Thank you to everyone who trusted me with their work.

With gratitude,

Cynthia Gellis
Editor - Rough Writers Anthology, 2019

MOMENTS IN
SPACE & TIME

Scientists say there are three

states of consciousness: awake,

sleeping and dreaming. Oh!

But consciousness is fluid.

Consciousness Will Ride

BY SUSAN CAMERON

After leaving the mating pond, leaving my seed behind just in case I do not survive, I make my way to the meditation area. My consciousness will ride faster than thought, leaving my watery world thru a portal to another world to join with another intelligent life form.

The admission clerk asked, "Just you?"
"Yes," I replied.
"That will be $5.75 for your visit today."
I pull out a crumpled wad of ones from my pocket and peel off six bucks, "keep the change."
The clickity click of my lone metal crutch echoes and bounces off the polished granite floor. I walk the length of hallways into the final antechamber that houses the exhibition gallery of the museum's Trompe l'oeil art. I often use the optical illusions of these three-dimensional visual trickeries to romp through the remembered adventures of my consciousness. I had found the most mind altering, beautiful and dynamic painting to use to enter an altered state of consciousness to aid in my journeys. The painting was a whirling mass of stars, nebulas and universes all revolving around a central star. It was an image of beauty and someplace I wanted to experience.
My crutch is a reminder of and aid to the sore hip from my last adventure. There I was a wolf trying to escape a rifle wielding rancher who thought I was killing his cattle. It was a case of mistaken wolf-dentity (the rancher seemed to think all wolves look alike). I was running and trying to outwit him, zigzagging the brush

covered landscape to stay alive. When I spied the outbuildings, I jumped through the broken, curtained window of one to hide in the darkest corner. I tried to make myself as small as I could, holding my breath, trying not to pant. The ranchers' boot heels rattled the rickety wooden porch and my nerves. The porch cricked and cracked under the weight of the hefty man who was carrying the gun with each boot step. Then he stopped, and his boots scrapped the floorboards as he turned to face the door I was hiding behind. The sound of the rifle being cocked filled my ears with death.

I watch in my mind's eye as yellow irises change to brown when I heard the Museum Guard, Eugene say, "Good morning Mr. McKnight."

I am yanked back from my mental musings, and startled, I almost shout hello. Instead, I regain my composure and acknowledge the guard's greeting with a nod of my head.

While remembering how I discovered and began these adventures, I thought about my current conundrum. I understand that the consciousness of this Oliver McKnight had joined with the wolf. The question is: did the person that I was become the container for the wolf's consciousness?

Scientists say there are three states of consciousness: awake, sleeping and dreaming. Oh! But consciousness is fluid. Time can be manipulated. Everything is energy and energy vibrates. There are so many other ways to enter a different timeline. Meditation, remote viewing, and drumming journeys are just a few of the modalities that I have used to enter into an altered state of consciousness.

Once again, I call my attention back from my musings to the painting which I have been trying to use as a gateway to another plane of being. *Focus on the painting, focus. Deep breath in, fill the lungs, breathe out all the air through an open mouth. Fill the belly with breath, breathe out. Repeat.*

After sitting here for hours, staring at the painting, my eyes just move around the painting from solar system to solar system.

I decide to call it a day. With that thought, my eyes snap shut and the consciousness that I am is gone into a place that is not here…a different time, a different solar system…

Before I open my eyes, I sniff, then stick out my tongue to taste the acrid, over-carboned puke of air of this strange world in which I find myself. Slowly I, Dagami, crack my eyes. I am staring at a huge painting of swirling galaxies. Don't panic, I tell myself, just watch and learn. Remember what the coterie of elders told me: I would have to work at being human. *Human*, my mind screams, as I look down, I say out loud, "what the HELL are these for?"

I hear a loud, "shhhhh!" I look left and then right to locate where the obnoxious hiss came from. The portal suddenly opens again, and the majority of my consciousness is pulled back. In route, I pass a consciousness who I will grow more familiar with over time. What did we learn? The body that was you, remembers when I was you.

I open my eyes to see that I am again sitting in front of the painting of swirling galaxies. Gasping for air after breathing water someplace else, I take a huge breath to over-compensate. I wonder if I forgot how to breathe this combination of oxygen and pollution. The museum guard asks if I am okay.

"Alright! Yes I am alright," I answer.

I stand with the aid of my crutch and grab my backpack in order to journey home. I need some time to sort out what I just experienced. I still feel him with me; all the way home on the transit, I mull over the eerie feeling that I am not alone here, inside my body.

Clickety! I am reminded, as I step in sync with my crutch.

I have arrived, summoned. But by whom? I can't believe I am here again in front of the museum. This is my fourteenth visit to view the painting. The problem is, it's three o'clock in the morning. I am too old for sleepwalking. I would call it zoned out but how can you zone out when you are in bed asleep? Now I am here in front of the museum, awake, contemplating how to get in, up several floors, and sneak around lights and alarms. I shake my head in disbelief that I am trying to figure out how to break into a museum that is closed.

I decide to go home, and as I turn to retrace my steps, I hear, "Good morning, Mr. McKnight."

It's Eugene, the guard from the museum, "a little early for a museum visit, isn't it?"

Feeling like I was caught in some diabolical plot, I answer with an embarrassed stammer, "I-I-I know, walking and thinking automatically brought me to here. I need to pay attention to where my feet take me. Good morning, Eugene."

I ask myself, why do I come? Maybe I'm hoping another portal will open and take all of him, my mind visitor, back to wherever he came from?

My crutch clicks to the bus stop. The bus is pretty empty at this time of the morning, there are just a few of us riding to get to our destinations before the sun cracks the veil of the night sky and the rest of the world competes for my attention and space.

As I sit on the bus, deep in thought, a quiet voice inside me says, "did you hear that?"

I did hear it, like an unconscious painful moan as flesh slapped flesh, somewhere in the back of the bus. I/he/we stick out our tongue to taste the air.

It tastes like blood and violence!

Quickly, I am up, crutch in hand, clicking to the back of the bus. There on the floor, huddled in the corner is a person in the fetal position, covering her head with one arm, trying to fend off her attacker with the other. Then I notice the attacker, welding a closed fist for his next blow. With a crack of my metal crutch to his wrist his fist goes limp. As the assailant howls in pain the cry signals the bus driver to slam on the brakes. I lung forward but catch myself on the nearest seat handles. The assailant flies over the bus seats, hops to his feet and runs for the back exit. Without thinking about it, I/he/we run after him.

He's gone! I somehow come back to my senses and mentally assault the other in my head with a barrage of angry questions and statements. What were you thinking? What do you think we were going to do? The guy was in his early 20's, my God, I'm almost a senior citizen. Why the Hell are you trying to make us into some kind of a superhero now?

With crutch in hand, I make it home before the sun comes up. Dagami and I have another argument about how to get him out of my head and back to his home.

Dagami screams out loud, "Listen! I'm not going back!"

Is it me, yelling at me? I feel like I am going crazy!

I hear him say, "When you opened the portal, my consciousness traveled down the pathway to you, forming us. We have merged together. We can't keep sitting in front of that painting hour by hour, day by day waiting for something to happen...desiring that stupid bologna sandwich on Wonder Bread for lunch. No wonder you can't go back and retrieve what you think you lost. You keep thinking about that damn sandwich!

"Look Oliver, you alerted us. If you had not made the starting efforts in front of the painting everything would have stayed the same, boring and filled with bologna sandwiches.

"When you went into an altered state of consciousness, Eugene stayed with you while you made all those attempts to off-planet."

"Who? What? Eugene? What are you talking about?"

"Eugene is there to alert the Union when there is an interested person viewing the *Union of Universes* painting.

"Eugene is what we call the caretaker, he is the museum guard. He has stayed in the museum chamber day after day while you practiced meditation or you fell asleep, and when you finally let your mind open and jump through the portal into another universe, he was there.

"Eugene had intuited your growing abilities. He alerted us to who was in the process of learning and trying. When you opened the portal, I Dagami, made ready to join with you.

"There are many like us from different areas of the solar system…to help with the transition. To raise you up! You opened the door to the *Union of Universes*. Will you answer yes or no to the evolution of your life?

"You need to be trained! Return this body to what it was in youth! Lean and sinewy muscle so that you can be quicker and stealth in action. No bologna where we are going.

"And your mind needs work, so that you really understand and know what you can do. After exercise comes Mind Flight School."

Here we are, locked in a dedicated room in my apartment. A digitized picture of the Multiverses is projected on the ceiling, walls, and floor, as our two minds, Dagami and Oliver, work together to become one as our consciousness bi-locate for the UU. Our body is here safe as our mind travels the universe.

Eugene has a key and takes care of this me/him/us, making sure the bills get paid and that we have something other than bologna sandwiches to feed this body as I practice opening the portal.

One day it finally opens. Slowly, I stand and walk through a portal. Poof just like that I am gone from this world. When I exit the other side of the portal, I am standing on a snow-covered mountain top looking down over the edge. No cold weather gear, no ropes for repelling down the mountain. I see broken bodies and death everywhere around me. It seems that the Union of Universes always has you in training or test mode. Now, how to get down without dying.

Just the beginning! ▪

How am I ever going to

find my way out of here?

Where would I go if I did?

Carl's Green Galaxy

BY CYNTHIA GELLIS

B ill never missed the gym on Wednesday mornings. Not because he was a gym rat, he rarely broke a sweat. He never missed Wednesday because that morning was the hot yoga class. It was Bill's favorite. The class was full of fit women in teeny, tiny shorts and sports bras bending and contorting into all sorts of exotic postures. He didn't take the class, but he had noticed that there was a certain treadmill with a direct line of sight to the yoga room. He would walk and contemplate the view.

Sometimes he would position himself awkwardly at the lockers in the hall so that any woman leaving class would have to squeeze past him. He had perfected the accidental rub up and would act surprised every time, *Oh, I'm so sorry!*

This gave him a chance to leer at someone's chest or crotch at close range. He liked to take a banana with him in his drawstring gym bag and would look for a girl to offer it to. It didn't often work, but man, did he get off when it did. That morning, he parked in his usual spot in the alley behind the liquor store next to the gym. He got out of the car and slipped his drawstring bag over his shoulders. Just as he was about to kick the door of his 2003 Dodge Neon closed an arm reached around his left side and grabbed the door.

"Hello Bill," breathed Hector, "I've been looking forward to meeting you in person."

The hair on Bill's neck stood straight up. It was the guy he had been laundering money for online. He tried to turn but Hector had him pinned between the car door and the frame. Not only had Hector noticed that Bill had his hand in the cookie jar, but he had been able to track him down.

"Look Hector, I have your money, I was just getting ready to Venmo it to you," Bill lied, gesturing to his phone. "It was part of the routing protocol check."

Hector smiled. His mouth was a slit, his eyes were steely daggers.

He nodded, "I'm sure it was Bill. But since I'm here, we're just going to go square things up now. You'll drive."

Bill got behind the wheel. He dropped his wallet and cell phone in the cupholder and took a deep breath. That's when he noticed that Jimmy, Hector's fixer, was sitting in the passenger seat.

Hector slid into the backseat. Bill could feel something pressing against his back. It reminded him of that horrible flight home from Austin last month, when the giant guy in the row behind him decided to take out his frustration with the in-flight service on the back of Bill's seat. Only Hector wasn't six foot seven and Bill was pretty sure that wasn't his knee.

They made their way across town, crawling through the morning downtown traffic. Hector was navigating, Bill driving, and Jimmy leaning threateningly over the center console. Jimmy never took his eyes off Bill.

The worst part about driving through downtown is the throngs of people who have decided that traffic laws don't apply to them. This phenomenon is particularly pronounced in the garment district, where it is not uncommon to find a train of garment racks jaywalking. When the sweatshop shifts change, the streets become virtually impassable as the night shift scurries to catch buses to their day jobs housekeeping on the Westside and the day shift scurries to clock in before their meager wages for the day are docked.

The shift change rush had nearly cleared, and Bill started to accelerate when a rogue frutas cart came racing across their path. When he slammed the brakes, the right side of Jimmy's face slammed against the dashboard and Bill noticed the menacing bulge in the back of his seat release. He realized that this was his chance.

Springing from the car like a cat escaping a bath, he threw himself into the crowd of seamstresses, bargain hunters, and frutas carts. He cut through alleys, avoiding main streets until he found himself in the heart of skid row.

Ducking inside an unoccupied tent, Bill sat down and tried to catch his breath. Rummaging through the occupant's belongings, Bill found twenty dollars, a Playboy magazine, and half a bottle of Old English 800. He downed the Old English in three efficient slugs and spent a few minutes contemplating the editorial perspective of the magazine before shrugging off his drawstring gym bag to tuck it inside with the banana.

When he unzipped the side pocket to put the cash in his wallet, he realized it was missing. So was his cell phone. A chill ran down his spine as he remembered that he had left them both in the cupholder when he jumped out of the car. He needed to get home to his computer so that he could deploy the poison pill. That was the only way he could purge the trails of his online activities before Hector discovered the real depth of his deception.

In a final sweep of the tent he found a pile of quarters. *Bus fair, yes!*

Two hours and twenty-seven minutes later, Bill was approaching his neighborhood. The 52 bus had let him off a little more than a mile from his apartment; he decided that he would rather walk than wait for the 151.

As he approached, he noticed that the door was wide open and a tsunami of dread washed over him. He heard Hector's voice and saw Jimmy seated in front of his computer.

"So, we've finished?"

"Yes. I've transferred everything to our Russian Bitcoin holding company. All that's left is to trigger the Co-Meritus hack from this IP and the FBI will take care of the rest."

Not only did these guys have access to all of his physical possessions, they had taken control of his virtual assets as well. There was enough in Bill's online presence for him to rack up a life sentence in federal prison without the incriminating extras Jimmy and Hector were planting there.

How could these guys have gotten the better of me? What am I going to do? His exit plan had always assumed that he could use his virtual identity to create a new life for himself in a hacker haven like Argentina or Vietnam, but he needed a passport and access to funds. Without a computer or his smart phone, he had no plan!

In a surge of self-preservation, Bill decided that he needed to put as much distance between himself and these guys as quickly as possible and began to retrace his steps down the stairs and out of the complex. He had enough change left to catch the 52 back downtown. There he could lay low until he figured out what he was going to do.

Bill paid his fare and proceeded to commandeer the center seat of the back row. As he sat down, he manspread and affected a posture that suggested he was asleep.

He needed to think. If he could get his hands on a couple grand, he could buy himself a new identity. *Who do I know who is flush with cash?*

Eventually, he nodded off. From his dreamless sleep he heard a commanding female voice, "Last stop buddy, time to go."

Bill startled awake. He blinked his eyes open and realized that it was twilight, that he was the only one on the bus, and that he had no idea where he was. The bus driver, intercom in hand, was glaring at him from the front of the bus.

"Where are we?" he asked groggily.

"At the end of the line for you."

"But…"

"You getting off on your own, or you want me to call the transit police to come get you?" she challenged.

His initial reaction was, *I'll show you what you can do with that radio, honey.* But the rush of adrenaline as he sprung to his feet woke him up enough to remember that he didn't want to call any official attention to himself.

"Oh, gosh! Sorry, yes, this is my stop!" he lied as he darted for the open back door.

Bill had barely stepped foot on the sidewalk when the door slammed shut and the bus disappeared down the lonely road. He wondered as he tried to take in his surroundings, *where am I?* There was an eight-foot fence topped with razor wire next to him. Behind it he could see a small parking lot and a warehouse. No business name or address numbers were visible.

Reflexively he reached into his drawstring gym bag for his phone so that he could ping his location. Slowly he withdrew his hand.

No phone, you idiot, he scolded himself.

According to the signpost, he was at the corner of Santa Fe Avenue and East 25th Street. He had seen an exit for Santa Fe Avenue off of the 405 freeway, but this was nowhere near a freeway. Now, the sun had completely gone down and he had no sense of direction in the dark. *How am I ever going to find my way out of here? Where would I go if I did?* He looked up at the sky.

There were few stars visible, a side effect of the smog and light pollution, but Bill picked out the brightest one he could find. He imagined an inhabitable planet orbiting that star, one full of nubile, sensuous women who would welcome him as a god and cater to his every whim. *Why hasn't anyone created an intergalactic transportation device? Can't they see that there is a planet full of women out there just waiting for me?*

He gazed in the direction that the bus had gone, wishing for it to come back. Then he turned around and began to walk in the opposite direction, hoping that it would lead him back to downtown.

After a few blocks, things started looking less bleak. There were more of the same unmarked warehouses surrounded by razor-wire topped fences, but some had market lights strung across the parking lots. He turned a corner. Murals covered the exteriors of all the buildings in a fenced-in compound. There were cars, music, and a taco truck. *This must be the arts district that Carl had been telling me about.*

Bill had known Carl since second grade. And while Bill considered himself too cool to have friends, Carl had always been unapologetically friendly to Bill. In fact, he called Bill yesterday to follow up on the invitation for his exhibit opening tonight.

"I know that you're really busy, but it sure would mean a lot to me if you could come," Carl said sweetly, "There will be loads to eat and drink and there should be plenty of pretty girls too, if you know what I mean."

Bill could feel Carl elbowing him in the ribs and winking through the phone. And even though drunk, art-scene girls would make easy pickings, he muttered something noncommittal.

"Great, I'll put you on the list!" Carl exclaimed.

Somehow, I managed to show up at Carl's art opening, what were the chances of that? He almost kept walking, but his stomach reminded him that Carl had promised there would be food and he reluctantly decided to listen to it.

There was a short line at the taco truck, but when he got to the front, the taco guy refused to serve him, "No wristband, no tacos buddy."

"Well, where do I get a wristband?"

The taco guy pointed to the far corner of the building where under a door illuminated by a single, bare lightbulb stood a luscious, 20-something year-old blonde with a clipboard and an attitude.

As Bill approached the clipboard girl, she eyed him up and down and shot a look to the man standing next to her who was roughly the size of a refrigerator. This girl could tell Bill was trouble from 50 yards. The refrigerator nodded. Bill was used to being aggressive and intimidating to girls to get his way, but her disdainful gaze and pet refrigerator made him feel very small as he approached. Clipboard girl was already on to his game.

"Can I help you?" she asked.

"Yeah, I need a wristband for the taco truck," he blustered.

"The taco truck is only for invited guests of the artist."

"Oh, but I AM a guest of the artist!" He took a step forward and leaned toward the clipboard.

The human refrigerator took a deep breath and flexed, which had the intended effect of getting Bill to step back.

"I'm sure," she rolled her eyes, sighed and held up her clipboard. "Name?" Suddenly the door popped open.

"Bill, you made it!" Carl exclaimed. "Kerry, he's with me! I'm so glad you made it man, come in, let's get you a drink!"

"Oh, but I just wanted to get a wristband for the taco truck first," Bill stuttered.

"You can get tacos later man, come check out my art, I am SO excited for you to see what I've been up to, it's going to blow your mind, you are going to love it, I know how into sci-fi stuff you are, this is going to be right up your alley…" Carl put his arm around Bill's shoulder and pulled him inside, deftly guiding him through the surprisingly crowded gallery to the bar, talking nonstop the entire time.

"My friend here needs one of our signature cocktails, my good man," Carl chortled confidently to the bartender with a wink.

The bartender winked back and moments later handed Bill a rather large, fizzy cocktail that appeared to be smoking.

Bill held the drink quizzically.

Before he could say anything, Carl began again, "Oh, don't worry, its just got a little dry ice in there for effect," he chuckled.

"By the way," Carl said, standing back and giving Bill the same once over that clipboard girl had. "Thanks for getting dressed up, man!"

Bill realized that he was still wearing his gym clothes from this morning and startled, began to fumble for some sort of excuse.

Carl cut him off, "That's ok man, I'm just so glad that you're here, I wouldn't care if you showed up in your gym clothes! Look, I've got to go find my agent, you have to meet her, she is brilliant. Sit right here and I'll be back in a sec!"

And just like that, Carl disappeared into the crowd. Bill realized that his mouth was open, and he wondered if he had said anything. Without thinking, he took a slug of the formidable cocktail that he was holding. Wow! That was some kind of drink.

He plopped down onto a bench, shrugged off his drawstring gym bag, and dropped it on the floor in front of him. He took a deep breath, then another gulp of the drink. Although he could feel the coolness of the liquid all the way down his throat, it was quickly followed by a fuzzy, warm feeling.

What am I going to do? I'll get Carl to help me! Carl could give me his passport and enough money to get out of the country. I can disappear to South America and start over.

Bill emptied his drink.

He sighed and looked up. It was the first time he noticed the artwork in front of him.

It was a green galaxy that filled his entire field of vision. He knew that this galaxy contained the planet that he imagined earlier. *All I really want is to be there.* The painting appeared to rotate and glow, its energy washed over Bill's body. He looked at his hands, they were radiating waves of green light. *What was in that drink!?*

He stood up, reaching toward the picture. *I have to touch it.* As he stepped forward, his feet got caught up in the drawstrings of his bag and he found himself falling. There was the loud sizzle of unchained electricity and he felt a charge run through his body. But he didn't crash into the painting, he kept falling, enveloped in pulsating green light.

Carl returned to find an Adidas drawstring bag on the floor in front of his green galaxy. There was no sign of Bill. ■

"The heir shall return,"

she foretold...

Prelude: Destiny's Heir

BY CHRISTOPHER GILDEMEISTER

t's beautiful, he thought. *I've lost it. But I'll get it back!*

Cody Wildstar stared at the galaxy that had been his home. The novas that glittered like crystal, the bands of nebulae that shone so brightly it almost hurt to look at them, the auroras of radiation bright as the sun, and the tiny planets so distant they were barely a flicker...

They had been his, once. The galaxy had been a playground for him to romp in – to dance among the stars as a Prince of Aeterbes and Heir to the Galactic order. Yet here he was now, with nothing to his name but his shining Star-Sled, now reflecting the cosmic glow above him, and the few meager possessions he had hastily shoved in his backpack. When the Zarnox had attacked his dynastic home of Aeterbes-Prime, Cody had wanted to stand and fight; but his father, the King, more concerned about the preservation of his progeny than of the planet he was sworn to defend, had ordered him to flee. And, hating himself every second, yet unwilling to defy his liege-lord and father, Cody had obeyed.

But even as his Star-Sled had soared into space, and the invaders had levelled his family's ancient fortress, shackled his father, and enslaved his people, the Oracle had uttered the prophecy: "The heir shall return," she foretold, "when Clophis rises in the green-banded sky."

Gazing at the single supernova dominating the concentric, emerald-hued rings in the cold dark aether above him, Cody knew: the time of his return was at hand. ■

Everybody know who I am. I'm the man.

Everybody knows that. But like I said,

you can't trust junkies.

A Question for Justice

BY TERRELL HARRISON

JUSTICE: Fairness. A state of affairs in which conduct or action is both fair and right, given the circumstances. In law, it more specifically refers to the paramount obligation to ensure that all persons are treated fairly. – Duhaime's Law Dictionary

When life is getting or has gotten too heavy, what do you do? How do you get away? And when you can't physically get away, how do you handle it? Suicide is not an option, at least not for me. What I do is mentally go back to the observatory, as weird as that may sound. I visualize myself at the observatory, staring into space. And from there I am able to escape into the universe, away from this place. It's a way not to be here and not to continue hashing over the attacks that are overwhelming me. Somehow, it's very soothing to imagine myself at the observatory, letting my mind drift into outer space. Well, for the moment anyway.

THE SITUATION

The police department planned a raid on a house known to be inhabited by drug dealers on East 32nd Street. However, the police responded to East 32nd Place, not East 32nd Street. The defendant in this case, Jordan Jefferson, who has been known to the police to be involved in the sale of drugs, happens to live on East 32nd Place.

Upon entering the house on East 32nd Place, an officer was allegedly shot and killed by Jefferson, who appears to have been the only occupant in the house at the time of the shooting. The other police on the scene were able to take

Jefferson into custody without further incident. There were no drugs found on the property.

JORDAN JEFFERSON

I was sitting at home watching television as I usually do on a Wednesday night. I don't go too far away from home anyway, because you can't trust too many people. I am known for dealing drugs in this town. Everybody know who I am. I'm the man. Everybody knows that. But like I said, you can't trust junkies. Nor can you trust your closest so-called friends EITHER. I don't know if I really have any real friends anyway. Everybody just hangs around to get what they can from me. And if I leave my place too long, they will rob me blind. So, I lay back and watch the tube, or listen to my jams with my honeys.

Why did I get into dealing? I'm a black man in a white town. Not very many opportunities to make any real money in the corporate world, because it's all rigged. Yeah, I had jobs. But I did better on the streets. I make up to three or four thousand dollars on a good day. How much do you make at your nine to five? And then you have to pay taxes and union dues and all those other fees and deductions the government takes out to keep you down.

You probably think I am dumb, uneducated, and have no skills. Yeah, I can see it in your eyes. You consider me a lowlife and want to lock me away forever just because I supply what the people out there want. If they didn't want it, I wouldn't have any business. And since they want it, why shouldn't I sell it to them? If I don't, someone else will. So, don't judge me.

But I am trying to get out of dealing. I'm tired of having to look over my shoulder everywhere I go.

Anyway, I'm not here on trial for drugs. I'm on trial for defending myself, and they want to call it murder. I was defending myself from a cop that was going to shoot me. I had to kill him before he killed me. Wouldn't you?

They broke into my place. MY PLACE! If I was dealing, I wouldn't keep contraband in my place. That would be amateurish and stupid. I am a professional at whatever I do. And later I found out that they had the wrong address anyway. Like I said, you never know what's going to happen in that neighborhood. So, I always keep my Glock within reach. And there they come breaking down my door.

THE TRIAL

My attorney supposedly did the best he could defending me, but I know he really can't truly feel what I have been going through. He's white. I'm not sure if I fully believe in him. But I realize that a black attorney won't do any good in this town. Here I am, a black man on trial for killing a white cop when HE broke into MY place.

Even though he didn't want me to get on the stand, I insisted. And after I got on the stand and swore to "tell the truth, the whole truth, and nothing but the truth," I told them exactly what happened. The prosecutor asked me if I knew the man was a policeman. I told him, "Of course I did. That's why I shot him."

"WHAT!?" he asked. "You are telling me that you knew he was an officer of the law?"

"Yes."

"How did you know that he was an officer?"

"He identified hisself when he broke into my door."

"And you shot him anyway," the prosecutor interjected.

"Hey man, slow your roll. I didn't have a choice."

He then said, "You always have a choice."

"NO! YOU have choices. You're white! I'm a black man in America trying to survive. We don't have the opportunity to make choices. Especially in situations like that."

"What is that supposed to mean?" he challenged.

"Man, a cop busts down my door and comes into my house yelling POLICE! When I heard the bump, outta reflex, I grabbed my piece and jumped up. He already had his gun in hand. If I had hesitated, I'd be dead."

"How many times did you shoot?"

"I don't know, man. I shot until he dropped!"

"Why didn't you just put the gun down?"

"Aw man, get the f*** outta my face."

"Why didn't you put the gun down when he identified himself?" the prosecutor pressed.

"I'm a black man with a gun. He's a white cop. I know his training has taught him that I was just a nigga with a gun that wants to kill him. How many brothas have been shot because they had a cell phone in their hand? Or a brush, or a book, or sometimes nothing? I shot because I don't want to be another statistic. If I was him and I looked up and saw a nigga with a gun pointing my way, I woulda shot me. Cops kill black kids for having ice cream in their hands and claim they felt they were in danger. Man shut the f*** up."

"Just calm down…"

"Naw man, don't tell me to calm down. I'm fighting for my life here. I was fighting for my life then and I am fighting for my life now. I did what any person would do in that situation."

"I wouldn't have shot a cop."

"And you would be a dead nigga."

"What?"

"Look, black people in this country get nervous every time they see a cop now. If we see a police car or hear about any situation that one of us has an encounter with a cop, it gives us reason to be concerned. I've seen where cops have shot the person that was trying to assist with capturing the so-called bad guy just because he was black. Black cops get shot by other cops, just because he was a black man with a gun. And yeah, he was in uniform. So what? I've seen a white guy swing an axe at a cop and ran right at the cop, acting like he was going hit him. The cops didn't shoot him, they tried to talk him into putting the axe down. And then he ran away. Yet, I saw a black woman with a screwdriver running away from a cop and he shot her and claimed she was a threat and he feared for his life. She was twenty or thirty feet away from him. Yeah, I shot the cop! Because I feared for my life. Is that a crime?"

"Shooting cops is against the law."

"So is shooting an innocent man," I countered.

"Your innocence is still to be determined."

THE DELIBERATION

Juror number one is a white businessman, mid-fifties. Number two: a white, retired postman, late sixties. Number three: a forty-something, white housewife. Number four: black plumber, mid-forties. Number five: black, female secretary, late fifties. Number six: thirty-seven-year-old male nurse, white. Number seven: white, male pharmacist, late-fifties who was later elected jury foreman. Number eight: black, male, sixty-eight-year-old retired salesman. Number nine: white, male security guard, about thirty. Number ten: fifty-year-old, black, male banker. Number eleven: forty-three-year-old, white, male realtor. And number twelve: white, male, seventy-year-old minister.

After a full day of deliberation, they weren't getting anywhere. All the jurors were tired and frustrated. They were locked at a vote of nine guilty, three not guilty. The foreman sent a message to the judge letting him know that they were deadlocked. The judge brought them back into the courtroom. He spoke to them about the importance of reaching a verdict and decided to allow them to rest for the night and start again in the morning.

The next morning, the first thing they did was have another vote. Still nine to three. After discussions and reviews of the testimonies, the white businessman, juror number one, said, "Well, we know who keeps voting not guilty."

Juror number ten, the black banker responded, "What's that supposed to mean?"

"You know what it means," declared juror number two, the white postman. "You people are always trying to cover up for each other. Just accept that he is guilty and let's get the hell out of here."

Juror number ten replied, "I'm not even going to entertain a response to that."

Number two: "It's simple, he said he did it. He's guilty."

Juror number six, another white man chimed in, "If it was all that simple, we wouldn't be here, would we?"

Number four, the black plumber, "He also said it was self-defense. And that's what we are here to determine."

Number three: "That's pretty convenient, don't you think? A drug dealer shoots a cop and then pleads self-defense. And you believe him just like that. We know how YOU voted."

"And we know how you voted. But at this point it's more about WHY you voted that way."

"What does that mean?" number three asked.

Number four responded, "Obviously you don't accept that it could possibly be self-defense. Again, I ask, why? Because it was a cop that was shot? Or because Jefferson is a black man?"

"Because he said he did it. And yes, because it was a cop... doing his job!"

"He was also in the wrong location, remember?" stated number twelve, the white minister.

"He was still doing his job. And if he hadn't gotten shot, he could have straightened the rest of that out. Anyway, why do you say he's innocent?" asked number nine, the white security guard.

"Look, I don't say that Jefferson is innocent," stated number ten, the black banker. "But I do say in this situation he is NOT GUILTY!"

"Wh-what? That makes no sense?" exclaimed number nine.

"That's because you live in different world."

"Of course, I live in a different world. I've never been a drug dealer."

"That has nothing to do with it."

"What do you mean, that has nothing to do with it? That's why the cops were there in the first place."

"NO! The cops were there because they went to the wrong address. Jefferson just happened to be an ALLEGED drug dealer."

"They got lucky," number three mumbled.

"What?"

"Never mind."

"No, no, no … THAT… that, right there tells me that you had him guilty right from the beginning," insisted juror number five, the only black female in the group.

"That's ridiculous."

"I wish it was ridiculous," juror number four, the black plumber, interjected. "But unfortunately, you can only see it from one side."

"Yeah, the right side."

"No… the white side."

"Sounds like you're calling me a racist or something."

"Not yet. But you are thinking as only a white man would think," said the black plumber.

"I'm white. What difference does that make."

"EXACTLY! You don't know what it means to be pulled over for driving while black. Or running while black or even walking while black. THAT'S THE DIFFERENCE."

"Huh?"

"Have YOU ever been stopped for a traffic violation?"

"Yeah, of course. Who hasn't?"

"Did they search your car?"

"Search my car? For what? It was a traffic stop!"

"What? The cops have you step out of your car? And search you, saying 'To be sure you don't have a weapon,' or drugs or whatever else they deem to be a reason to search you?"

"No, of course not. I don't give them any reason to feel that they need to search me."

"Do I look intimidating?" juror number ten, the black banker asked.

"No, I wouldn't say that you do."

"Yet each time that I was stopped I had to," he made air quotes, "'Step out of the car and be checked/searched for OUR safety.'"

One of the black jurors yelled out, "What if it was your son who was in the same situation and saying he shot a cop in self-defense. Would you believe him?"

"First of all, my son wouldn't be in that situation," juror number one responded.

"Do you all feel that your son couldn't possibly be in that situation?"
Most of the white jurors said, "Yes, of course." Others made no comment but looked surprised that anyone would try to turn it around like that.

The white pharmacist stated, "My son has been stopped by the police on various occasions and has never had a gun pointed at him. I'm not saying he is any kind of angel or anything, but he has never put himself in such dangerous situations."

Number eleven, the white realtor then added, "If that Jefferson guy had been raised properly, he would have known better than to pull a gun on an officer of the law."

Juror number eight, the sixty-eight-year-old, black, retired salesman, finally jumped in, "If you will indulge me for a moment. I think I can help to explain what this young man is trying to say."

"Will this help this case?" asked juror number eleven. "Because I am tired of this whole argument and tired of being here."

Number eight responded, "Yeah, we all are. But please, hear me out. And yes, I think it will at least bring us to a better understanding of each other and possibly show you a view from another perspective, so to speak."

"Yeah, whatever," mumbled number eleven.

"I have to ask all of you ... how do you feel, when the police arrive on the scene?"

They all had various responses. Some gave answers such as "relieved," "they will straighten it out," "I'm fine with it." Some said, "I get nervous," "there's going to be more trouble," "somebody's going to jail," "scared."

"Now I want you to note that the more positive responses came from those of you that are of ... uh the lighter persuasion. But from the people of color came the unsure, more nervous and even scared responses. Why is that?"

"I'm sure you're going to tell us," someone quipped.

"We all want to believe in the police motto: to protect and serve. But we don't all have that experience. You might think that race relations in America has improved. A couple of you probably don't give a damn. I, as a black man, have experienced a different relationship. I dare to say that most people of color, especially blacks, will say that things are not only no better, but worse now than they were years ago in many cases. When I was young, I did a lot of stupid things that I would get shot for today. These days, I've seen too many cases where black men, women, AND CHILDREN get shot and killed by the police that showed up to PROTECT AND SERVE. And the cop's claim is that they feared for their lives. Now in this case I am not trying to tell you how to vote. Nor am I saying Jefferson probably shouldn't be off the streets. But if you are going to convict him, convict him for the right reason. I am wondering if anyone remembers, or ever knew what it means, when you say in the Pledge of Allegiance to the flag: WITH LIBERTY AND JUSTICE FOR ALL."

THE VERDICT

After what seemed like forever, the jurors file back into the courtroom. My throat is so dry, I can hardly swallow. What did they decide? Are they going to burn me? My attorney doesn't look very confident. I'm probably going away for the rest of my life. But if they are doing their job right, they should find me "not guilty." I am not guilty of murdering that cop. Yes, I shot him, but I had no choice.

I close my eyes and sit here, again visualizing my "getaway place." Looking at all those stars, I wonder *are there planets around each star?* That would mean that there are more planets in the universe than stars, that we can't count. Wow! *How many of those are like earth? How big are they? What is the possibility of life out there?* LIFE... WOW. Speaking of life; here comes the jury.

The Judge addressed the jury and asked, "Mister Foreman, have you reached a verdict?"

"Your Honor, we the jury ...."

What would be your desired outcome in this case? More importantly... WHY?

THE END?

"When you're accustomed to privilege, equality feels like oppression."
- Clay Shirky ■

Dean drew in his last breath and
closed his eyes, waiting for the
end to come.

Departing

BY BENJAMIN THOMAS HORAK

Traveling, in some ways is like practicing your own death. When the time comes, you say goodbye to your loved ones, put on your Sunday best, then cram yourself into a tight metal cylinder and wait to be shoved off into an underworld of collapsing space and time; all the while hoping, no - praying, to arrive in a state of splendor, joy, and renewal.

Dean Pratt, a young and nervous man, dodged giddy travelers as he made his way to the station waiting area. There he slowly searched for his assigned seat and upon finding it in row E7, seat number 56, a frown of disappointment grew on his face. His log of a body fell into the red cushioned chair, exhaling with a fretted sigh that went on and on and on.

Pulling off a small backpack that was pinned between the seat and his back, he threw it on the floor near his feet as if no longer wanting the burden of it. Dean tried to calm himself.

"I can do this," he said to himself, "I can do this," repeating the mantra in his head and under his breath as his body sank further into the seat.

"Excuse me, is this row E7, number 55?" asked an elderly woman. She was no bigger than a pea and just as shriveled.

Dean bolted upright, "No!" he yelled, but one look into the old woman's sincere eyes, his cheeks flushed red. "Yes, sorry, this is the right seat."

He stood up to offer his own, as he was taught in school, only to watch the women gently sit in the adjacent chair. She didn't seem to notice his awkwardness.

"Are you here alone?" she asked. "You're not traveling with someone?"

Dean shook his head and sat down. Fixing his eyes outward across the waiting area he noticed a pink-haired child dash into and then out of view, dragging her mother into the crowd. A marquee sign winked updates of arrived, departed, arrived, departed, arrived, departed.

"For the love of god, why can't it say canceled," said Dean.

"What? The Zeilinger is canceled?" asked the woman. Her head snapped upwards towards the marquee, gripping her chest in a panic.

"No, sorry," said Dean. He glanced down to the backpack at his feet, "I just want it to be canceled."

"First time in a Zeilinger?" she asked.

Dean nodded. He had never traveled across the galaxy. Zeilinger station was sixty miles above his home, the red desert planet of Okamboo. With a direct teleport to Earth, it was the only option for a trip he had not planned to take.

"Well there is nothing to it, you won't feel a thing," she smiled and patted his knee. That assurance gave some relief to Dean.

"My name is Hannah," she said.

"Dean," he replied.

They both smiled as Hannah's husband stormed in and took a seat next to Hannah. "I can't believe it!" he said. "They don't sell beer at the bar! They serve coffee, black tea, wine, tequila, vodka and those disgusting Bloody Marys. The server wanted to get me to try fermented oxygen...what the hell is fermented oxygen?"

"Calm down," said Hannah. "This is Dean. Dean this is my husband, Willis."

"Hello," said Dean, giving a faint wave of his hand and trying out a smile that wound up as thin as a toothpick.

Willis gave a nod to Dean and said, "Do you have any beer?"

Hannah put her elbow into Willis's side. He jumped a little from the pain. She was small, but she knew where all the soft spots were.

"Behave," she said with a scolding tone.

"I'm a retired sculptor," said Willis.

He stretched out his left hand. Awkwardly, Dean reached over Hannah to grasp it. Willis had a coarse, dominating grip that tightened over Dean's hand as if it had something to prove to the world.

"So," said Willis, finally releasing Dean from his threatening grip, "what brings you out to Zeilinger station?"

Dean tried to hide the pain in his fingers, rubbing his hand like a pet dove. "I'm going," he began to say, then stopped. Choosing his words carefully, he continued, "to deliver a family heirloom."

"We are going to see our grand-daughter's graduation," smiled Willis.

Eager to move the conversation away from himself, Dean asked, "What's her degree in?"

"Philosophical systems," said Willis. "What the hell can you do with a degree in philosophical systems?"

"Uh..." Dean didn't have an answer. He worked in robot repairs.

"Correct, nothing," said Willis.

Hannah jabbed her elbow into his side producing another yelp.

"So, you're a sculptor? What do you sculpt?" asked Dean.

"Stone," said Willis.

"Yes, but ..."

"He makes the most emotional figures. In marble," said Hannah.

"Yeah, well I did it for 60 years of my life. I'm retired now, traveled too much ya know?" Willis gruffed with a gentle frown.

"Too much?" asked Dean, shifting uncomfortably in his chair. He was not sure that he wanted to hear the answer.

"Yeah. Got a red card now, have to sign my life away every time I use the Zeilinger." He held up his passport, revealing the alarming bright red cover, the result of years of transport radiation. The station would not allow him to travel commercially without a signed liability waver.

Dean looked down at his own passport, dangling below his neck at the end of a lanyard. The bright green cover glowed like spring leaves. A dead give-away that he had never departed from a Zeilinger.

"You see, once you go red," Willis said with a grin, "the radiation starts to affect your genes, and you'll get mutations."

"Mutations? What mutations," asked Dean gripping the arm rests like a vice.

Willis widened his grin until it resembled a freshly carved jack-o-lantern.

"Well, I'm right-handed," he said as he brought his right hand out for Dean to see, like a leviathan emerging from the depths.

Willis's hand was a monster. A mutation of fingers fused together and curled inward like a claw; it shook like a shaggy wet dog.

"Oh my god!" Dean squealed.

"Yeah, you better not get a red card," Willis shoved Dean's shoulder with his deformed hand. "It will ruin you good boy!"

"Willis you are scaring the boy!" shouted Hannah.

She retracted Willis's hand with both of her arms into the depths of her lap, never to be seen again. Dean continued his bewildered stare at the now hidden claw, terrified it would return.

A flash of pink hair marched across the row of seats, "Mommy, we are here!" an excited seven-year old girl exclaimed. It was the same girl who had been towing her mother through the crowd earlier.

"Hello," said the girl cheerfully.

When Hannah removed her hands from Willis's claw to wave hello, the girl's eyes widened in shock.

"Why does your hand look like that?" said the girl, slowly climbing into her seat.

"Chloe!" scolded her mother. "What did we say about talking to people?"

Chloe looked down at her pink shoes. "Sorry," she whimpered.

"I got the red card, girl. My hand is deformed from traveling," said Willis, brandishing his crimson passport. He smiled; he was almost proud of scaring little girls with his claw.

"Deformed," Chloe said the word with a clarion tone. Her face scrunched into a ball, her hands dropped to her side and her back straightened against the labor of spelling the word out. She formed each consonant and vowel as if pulling from a hunk of wet clay and shaping them with the crude, but effective palette knife of her lips, "D-E-F-O-R-M-E-D, deformed." She inhaled deeply from the effort, then gave a small bow.

"Very good honey," her mother said with a proud smile. "We are on our way to compete in the spelling bee nationals on Earth."

"Is that right? I was a spelling bee champion when I was her age," said Willis.

"Really when was that?" asked Chloe.

Willis leaned back slowly, recalling the years of his childhood. "Oh well, that would have been ninety years ago."

"Wow, that's a long time ago. You are very ancient," said Chloe, with a smirk. "A-N-C-I-E-N-T, ancient."

Willis leaned into Hannah and whispered in her ear, "Do you think we could stuff her in an airlock?"

Her response was an elbow to his side.

"Oh, you have a bright green passport like me!" shouted Chloe as she put her passport next to Deans. "We're twinsies!"

"Ha what?" Willis leaned over to meet Dean eye to eye. "You have never departed on a Zeilinger? How old are you?"

"This is his first time departing. He is very nervous and you're not helping," said Hannah.

"First time departing, no wonder he looks so pale. This whole time I thought you were a vegan!"

"Willis!" shouted Hannah.

"Vegan, V-E-G-A-N, vegan."

"That's good girl," said Willis. "Now can you use it in a sentence?"

"Dean is a vegan because he is pale," said Chloe.

"See! From the mouths of babes," Willis threw up his hands for support.

"I'm not vegan! I'm not vegan!" shouted Dean. "I'm I'm..."

"Nervous," smiled Hannah, patting Deans thigh. "There is nothing to it, you won't feel a thing."

The comfortable smile relaxed Dean. He wished Hannah was his grandmother. He didn't grow up with one, but if he had, maybe his life would have been a lot better.

"No Pain? Ha!" said Willis. "The moment they scan your atoms and entangle 'em with some inert gas 20,000 light years away is the moment they smash your atoms into oblivion, making a carbon copy of you on the other side of the galaxy in one big green poof. Say *sayonara* to the original you!"

Willis was cackling with pleasure; he was enjoying himself way too much. Hannah's scolding frown did little to ruin his fun.

"My uncle has a red card," added Chloe. "He went on a Zeilinger and came back with his eyeballs stuck in his stomach."

"Is that so?" said Willis. "I guess a man can feast on sight alone."

Dean's hands went numb with panic, his chest contracted, forcing all the air from his lungs. Clutching his throat, he croaked out desperate words which were drowned in sobs.

"Oh god, I think he's suffocating!" shouted Hannah.

"Eh, let 'em, builds character."

"Suffocating, S-U-F-F-"

"Stop! Stop it!" screamed Dean, collapsing to the floor. "I don't want to die in a green poof!" His body twisted violently on the smooth station floor. The sudden jerks opened his backpack, releasing its contents: a small cylindrical container.

It rolled across the floor and bumped into Willis's boots.

"What's this?" asked Willis, picking up the silver container to inspect it. His claw traveled across the surface of the canister, reading each small groove and depression. In that moment, Willis was again a sculptor, feeling a block of marble to discern the image within before the first hammer strike.

"A sarcophagus," said Willis.

"My mother's ashes," heaved Dean. Still on the ground, he rolled onto his back catching his breath.

Willis was finally silent for once. He continued to move his hands over the cylinder, feeling the subtle curves of the metal. The sarcophagus had sparked a painful, old memory, something he longed to forget.

"I'm sorry about earlier, I was just pulling you around," said Willis quietly. He was almost apologizing.

"You like to mess with people, I get it. You would have liked my mother, she messed with my whole god damn life," Dean said, the panic shifting to anger.

Getting up from the floor, he snatched the canister from Willis's claw and dropped it into his backpack. The once lively row went silent. Dean settled back into his chair, fuming.

The station's marquee continued to flash travel updates while more excited travelers filled the waiting area. The Zeilinger departure was soon approaching.

"I have to ask something," said Dean, keeping his focus on the crowd. "When I depart, am I going to meet her?"

He took the sarcophagus from his bag, looking it over like a child inspects a splinter. Nobody in row E7 said a word.

It was a curious thing, teleportation. The atoms are instantly replicated at the destination, but the traveler's consciousness lingers in a bodiless void. The phenomenon is made worse when traveling with the remains of the deceased. Fragments of consciousness still cling to the remains, even after cremation. During the process of teleporting, it is not uncommon to see your dead mother arise from the big sleep and start talking to you about how your life is a waste, why you will never be successful, and why can't you be like your brother with a wife and two kids.

"Of course," said Hannah, squeezing her face into an adorable smile. "Wouldn't that be delightful?"

Dean slumped into his chair.

"I hated my mother. She controlled every aspect of my life, what to eat, what to say. She never once praised me. Not once. I was never good enough for her. When she died, I didn't feel sad, I felt relief." Tears flooded his sunken eyes, "I never want to see her again, but the family on Earth wants her remains sent back, and they want me to attend the funeral."

Willis leaned out from his seat. "Can't you just stay here? Fuck your relatives, right?"

Dean didn't reply immediately. This question had raced through his mind all day. But it was his obligation to go. Sending a sarcophagus through the quantum mail would be insulting enough to the family. Not attending his own mother's funeral would give rise to rumors that he had become like her, crazed with rage.

"I never thought that once she was gone, she would come back from hell to haunt me," he said.

Hannah reached over and pulled Dean into her, "I'm so sorry, I didn't know."

Willis put his claw-hand on Dean's shoulder.

The announcement from the station stated the Zeilinger was ready for boarding. A commotion of excited travelers began to line up to enter the great sphere of a machine. Dean's body shook but his anger was slowly fading. Hannah held his arm and patted his palm to calm him.

Thirty minutes later, it was his turn to go. He stepped into the Zeilinger, a massive, white, spherical womb of a structure. The floor vibrated as quantum computers scanned his atoms, churning computations of nature beyond the human limits. Dean was about to face his limits. For the sake of a family who never loved him.

But it would be over. A desire of hope filled his chest. He would have a new beginning on a blue and green planet, his copied atoms experiencing life for the first time. He wondered if his senses would change as well. Would he feel cool breezes differently? Would the smell of salt on the ocean be sweeter? Would the warmth under a yellow sun sooth his skin? This was the joy that Dean hoped for: the release from the pain of a red desert world.

The Zeilinger hummed into a crescendo of clamorous noise. Dean drew in his last breath and closed his eyes, waiting for the end to come. The flash was more intense than expected as his atoms collapsed into an after-glow of rippling currents of radiation. Traveling now through an underworld of collapsing space time, his mind was changing into something new.

A figure was with him, a small, old woman. She wore a plain, white dress, soiled with blood. Dean looked into her stern face and saw the end of his old life. She opened her mouth to speak, but he did not listen. Dean had finally departed. ■

Now, looking into this approaching

brightness, I felt that old darkness.

Moving Lights

BY CARY KELLEMS

R UN...RUN...Run...run.
Fear screamed through my mind with a desperation akin to the undulating death throes of a bludgeoned baby seal. A scream that skittles unimpeded across the white nothingness of an arctic ice sheet.

RUN was telegraphed from every single goosebump on my body.

"Run, run...run little brother..run!"

But my body would not respond. The electrified penumbra of this oncoming luminous apocalypse permeated my very core with dread. A dread I had felt a thousand times before.

My childhood dreams were often interrupted by the nocturnal dread of my drunken and belligerent father. A man of great girth and temper whose capricious rage was like a rattling, spinning wheel of misfortune. Each of his daughters and each of his sons frozen in their beds by the suspense of who of would be the unlucky candidate for the belt. With nowhere to run, I could feel the dread permeate from my sisters' room while my brothers and I dined in darkness on the fear of being hurt by someone we so desperately wanted to love.

Who would it be tonight? Which one of us had committed some unknown transgression that would warrant a swift but arbitrary punishment? Corporal punishment from a drunken father. A father who we loved when he was sober. But even during those times, we still feared him.

As the commotion from the living room grew, we knew that this passion play would soon reach its climax. With bright eyes in our dark room, my brothers and

I waited and waited and waited until that moment when our door swung open, flooding our dark room with the garish light from the hallway.

My mind would scream, *"RUN, RUN...Run...Run."*

But I could not move.

Now, looking into this approaching brightness, I felt that old darkness. At this moment I was again reliving a lifetime of running. Running from the fear and dread that dwelt within the light, be it the garish light of the hallway that exposed three young boys, or this swirling mass before me now. This electrifying, yet familiar, visceral dread that was vomiting through my body suddenly and completely stopped. For the first time in my life, it had stopped!

The reflexive desire to run instantly coagulated into an iron will to stand. To stand against the burly beast who was waiting in the hallway with a belt in hand. To stand against the devasting, swirling force before me. An energy that might tear me to shreds yet could no longer motivate me to run. This irresistible force had finally meet an immovable object.

So, as I stood, ready to face the darkness within the light, a wry smile grew across my face and I waited. Waited to confront that darkness. Waited to address my own personal apocalypse. ∎

Although an exact science, all

the numbers presented herein

are approximate...

Conscripted Space

BY JAMES KINSTLE

C onventional wisdom has told us that prostitution is the oldest profession in the world. But, of course, that is not true. The oldest profession is actually the "bait and switch." In the interest of transparency, to analyze this tech-nic-ology can be served by merely pointing it out where it exists, so that the recipient is not misled by the flim-flam man.

In an unusual turn of events I have been asked to temporarily be that man: the flim-flam man. By accepting the premise that the cover for the booklet I was hired to write is representative of the booklet's subject matter, I have to begin by talking about the bait before transitioning into the booklet's real purpose.

Please look again at the cover, again, while I tell you what the bait is: the bait is "oouh and aah," a phony picture of astronomy of which I know very little about. There is no table of contents because the reader has to be swept away. You have to use your imagination to pretend temporarily that you are an occupant of a parallel universe without knowing what a parallel universe is to grasp simple facts about space in this instruction to astronomy.

Although an exact science, all the numbers presented herein are approximate and shape shifting has been employed to present the concept of space (SPACE), or deep space if you prefer.

START:

The hydrogen atom has a proton at its center and an electron buzzing around it. If the proton were the size of a dime (ten cent coin) the electron would be about a mile away. In between is nothing: empty space.

Nobody knows what physical size an electron is. If you discovered a proton dime found on the sidewalk in Belmont Shore, CA, you would have to ride a bicycle or take the city bus halfway to Seal Beach to look for the corresponding electron.

Nobody knows what gravity actually is, other than it seems to hold everything together, somehow.

If the sun were the size of a dime, the earth would be about six and a half feet away. And the earth would be the size of the ball of an extra fine ballpoint pen.

Again, if the sun were the size of a dime, the nearest other star would be three hundred and forty miles away. For a sun coin found in Belmont Shore you would have to drive or fly up to Monterey or maybe Santa Cruz to look for the dime sized other star laying around waiting for you to see it.

Still again, if the sun were the size of a dime in "our" galaxy shrunk down to match the sun dime size, the nearest other galaxy would be about one hundred and sixty million miles away, with nothing, I am told, in between but empty space.

Light Photon – if you watched the sun send out of packet of light to the Earth, you would have to watch for eight minutes while it moved along the line until it got to the Earth. Light always travels the same (and fastest) speed in empty space.

Your human eye can only see a tiny, tiny part of all the light there is.

Black Holes are mysterious, dark objects in space that suck in (absorb) light, and stars, and planets, etc.

SPACE:

There are about four billion people on the earth.
There are about four hundred billion stars in "our" galaxy.

There are about four hundred billion galaxies in the universe.

SIDE NOTES:

Global Warming – if the earth could be moved a little bit further away from the sun, it would cool off a little bit.

Forever unanswered question – where does God live? ∎

Is this a test? I asked myself. Am I
ready for every possible question?

Greenlight Go!

BY DAVID KITCHEN

D o you ever think about those moments that you couldn't wait for something to be over? Sometimes the anticipation can be overwhelming. Even though it is just a brief moment, it feels like an eternity. I often encounter these moments, but nothing like the one some years ago. I remember it like it was yesterday.

There I was, sitting and waiting for that little light to turn green. It was kind of unusual to have a light signal at this particular location. I guess there was a need to let people know when it was their turn to go. It seemed like it was taking so long. I definitely felt like I was sitting at the longest red light ever. I still think about the time spent waiting for that little green light and how the thoughts swirling through my mind began to overwhelm me. Was this really the best time for introspection?

I was just staring out the window when out of nowhere the guy in the black and white appeared. He seemed to be a little short, perhaps because I could barely see his upper torso through the window. I couldn't see if he was wearing a badge, but I knew he was looking at me. *Oh geez*, I thought. *Where did he come from?* I was hoping everything was in order.

Another minute passed. I was still waiting for that stupid green light. *Is he going to signal for me or what?* I thought to myself. And, *what could be taking the officer so long?* It seemed like I was waiting for an eternity. I recall slowly reaching for my pockets to ensure that I had my identification. My shirt was buttoned properly, my tie was on straight, and I looked professional. There was no reason to cause any suspicion that things were not in order.

It was quite a busy location. I saw a deli window to my right. *There are so many people here,* I pondered. Even though the deli was bustling with people coming and going, I could not have felt more alone. It was just me and my thoughts, sitting there, waiting my turn. Mentally, I rehearsed all the right moves; how to introduce myself; how to retrieve my identification card; how to make eye contact and speak firmly and assertively. I practiced in my head, *Yes sir. No sir. Here you go sir.* Afterall, I rarely had an opportunity to meet face-to-face with an officer for this reason. I could still see the guy in black and white through the window. I continued to wait.

My mind began to play tricks on me.

I heard a voice sing out, "where is Kitchen?"

"That's me," I jumped.

Here we go. My hands were shaking, my mouth was dry. I felt a nervous smile expand across my face. *I am ready,* I told myself. With my stomach churning and my palms sweating, I looked toward the window. *Wait a minute. Darn it!*

What I thought was someone asking, "where is Mr. Kitchen?" was merely someone in front of the deli asking, "where is <u>the</u> kitchen?"

Oh, my goodness! I was definitely suffering from selective hearing. This was the longest I had ever waited for a greenlight.

I rehearsed what to do again in my head. Out of everybody here, he was singling me out; I needed to be prepared.

I mumbled to myself, "I have my ID. Be cool. Wait it out."

I reminded myself to stop checking my watch and ditch the cell phone! I went through the seven must-do things: be ready, acknowledge the officer, stay calm, show competence, don't make any sudden, erratic movements, keep my answers short, and be sure to say thank you.

Is this a test? I asked myself. *Am I ready for every possible question?*

I just needed to demonstrate how well I could follow directions. With my astute communication skills, this face-to-face encounter should be short. I was sure the officer would let me go through and not detain me too long.

Suddenly, there it was. That annoying light changed from red to green. I thought to myself, *OK, here we go!*

I heard a different voice this time, "Kitchen. David Kitchen."

This time it was not someone looking for a kitchen. This time someone was actually calling my name. I gazed around and unwrapped my fingers from around the black seat cushion that I was nervously gripping so tight. I stood up, walked forward past the deli, and approached the window.

"Good morning, sir," I said, so glad at not having to wait any longer. "I'm David Kitchen. Here are my identification and documents."

The portly gentlemen, dressed in a clean white shirt and solid black tie, with his pocket badge affixed so perfectly and eyes piercing through me from the other side the window, snatched my documents impatiently. He gave them a perfunctory glance, then handed them back.

"Everything appears to be in order Mr. Kitchen," he confirmed. "You are cleared to move forward. You will be meeting with the communications compliance officer about the manager position here at the Los Angeles Times. Be mindful of the time," he instructed. "the compliance officer has with a very tight schedule. Good look on your interview!"

Finally!

I smiled to myself, *I am interviewing with one of the top officers.*
I can still remember that carnival of nerves feeling. It actually felt like waiting at a red light, wondering if I was going to be pulled over by an officer of the law. I was very glad that it was a different kind of officer. It was my first interview for a manager position with a fortune 500 company. Wow! It sure seemed like the longest wait ever. What a sense of relief I felt when I could say to myself, "Just be cool, I got the green light. Go!" ■

When I see the green and white
light, I remember that I am a
visitor of peace and joy.

I Am Here 4 U

BY LOLA! LOVE

first remember being here in the early 1950's although it seems like I've been here forever. I feel that my assignment was to stay for a few years, to study, innovate, and move-on. Yet I have no idea how long I have truly been here unless I use the primitive, linear time system that these beings use here on this planet.

My time here is about to end; I can feel it. I see the messages in the green and white light everywhere I go! When I look into the light, I see my rich, loving, and vibrant planet calling me back. I want to go back but something is holding me here. Something that I can't describe. Something that keeps telling me, there's more to be done here, you can't leave now. However, the longer I stay, the weaker I become.

The creatures that inhabit this planet are like nothing I've ever experienced in all of my travels; and I have traveled to many galaxies. I sometimes feel like I'm lost because I wake-up each day wondering, *what am I doing here in this foreign, fraudulent, and fatal place?* When that happens, I begin exploring my energy field to find out who I am, where I am, and why I came to this place. Suddenly my objective and my purpose for being here becomes clear. When I see the green and white light, I remember that I am a visitor of peace and joy. I have come here to assist the confused, clueless, and consciously unaware creatures on this planet to be more compassionate, more loving, and more mindful of their planet and its inhabitants. However, my thoughts and actions become opaque and senseless when I have strayed from my purpose. When I get caught up in the tempo of their frenetic energy, I become so helpless that I capitulate to the influence of my surroundings. I begin to feel misplaced, disoriented, and powerless. Yet I asked to come here and I am determined to experience, to learn, and to leave this place joy-filled and in alignment with the planet's divine purpose.

Right now I am weary from the cacophonous, chaotic, and catastrophic environment created by the inhabitants of this planet and I feel lost and unsure of completing my assignment. The egregious, perilous, and unsettled energy that is vibrating here on this celestial body feels ominous and is unequivocally apocalyptic.

But something keeps me here, something that I can't describe. Something that feels so powerful that I remain here, helplessly lost in space. Sometimes I feel invisible. As if I am lost in the fourth dimension of time with no way home.

This familiar and unwelcome feeling happens every time that I sit to contemplate my reasons for coming to this tumultuously beautiful planet. Then, like divine intervention, I am soothed once again by my life support. This recurring and intermittent directive appears as green and white light and fills my spirit with joy. I see green and white hearts with arrows, and stars twinkling intermittently. At the center is always a beautiful, radiant, shimmering, gold and white brilliance that's pulling me, drawing me, reminding me to complete my mission so that I can return home.

When I get very still and allow my essence to connect with this image, my vision becomes dramatically vivid and I see impressive and energetic images of many luminescent and colorful beings. Animated, beautiful spirits dancing, laughing, singing, and playing. Yes, I can see the nature of my existence, the divinity of my complexion, the survival of my soul. I am slowly remembering and longing for where I've come from. When I feel this power overtaking my being, I delight in the joy, in the light, and I feel green and white all over. I believe it starts vibrating from my backpack. It's like I am carrying my personal life support on my person and it keeps me from dying. It keeps me from slipping into the unnatural rhythm of this out of sync and falsely fabricated place. Yet I always end up here with these thoughts running through my mind, not knowing if it's a diabolical dream or my destiny.

I was exhausted, that's why I sat down on this bench. However, the replaying of the benevolent reminder of my merciful mission has refreshed, revived, and reprogramed me to vibrantly continue my assignment here, on planet ZenEarth. ∎

...it all came pouring out of the

image and into his consciousness.

The Substitute

BY LYDIA MARTINEZ

After everything he had been through, George couldn't believe that he was right back where he started; in the middle of his family farm, looking at the sky, and wishing he was anywhere but there.

The dark night skies and the northern lights shimmering across the lake and grasslands had been the fodder of many dreams. George wanted to be an artist. He dreamed of capturing the beauty of where he had grown up and the places that he had only read about in books.

But his father had other plans for him. His father wanted to pass his farming knowledge along to George to keep the farm, the legacy of their family, going even as many other farmers were moving on to greener pastures in the city.

Every morning, George would get up at five o'clock to do the many chores that come with being the only son of a farmer: feeding and watering the animals, mucking the barn, splitting firewood. The work was hard and endless. He rushed through his chores as fast as he could because he could only go to school if they were done. School was where George felt he had a chance to be the person he wanted to be, an artist, a photographer.

George grabbed his camera and ran to catch the school bus. If he missed the bus it was a two-mile walk to the school and he would be late to the only class he was interested in: photography. Photography class this year was particularly exciting; the regular art teacher, Mrs. James, was out on medical leave and the substitute, Mr. Lanting, was a photographer who was regularly published in *National Geographic*. Mr. Lanting had traveled the world and was here in the middle of what felt like nowhere. George couldn't believe his luck. He was determined to learn everything he could from Mr. Lanting, who quickly became George's idol.

One of the assignments that Mr. Lanting gave the students was to photograph what they saw everyday but to put it in a new light. George was eager to start this assignment; after all, it was a chance to show the passion and enjoyment he felt while learning to be a good photographer. It was a chance to show how good he had become at the technicalities of photography, lighting, composition, color and how to vary the settings of his camera, all while still discovering his photographic style and voice. While George was doing his morning or night chores, he would stop to take pictures of the animals. Even though he took care that the lighting was good and the composition and form captured what he was trying to say, he was quickly becoming discouraged because in his mind the pictures looked like any other photographs of farm animals.

On the day the assignment was due George meekly turned in his portfolio, sure he had failed. "I see these animals every day. I tried everything I could think of to put them in a new light, but there is nothing special about them."

Mr. Lanting stopped what he was doing and looked up, "George, what may be ordinary and every day for you may be a new and refreshing way for someone else to view the animals."

George shrugged his shoulders and walked back to his desk with his head down, sure he had failed at the only thing he ever wanted to be good at.

That evening Mr. Lanting was reviewing the students' portfolios. As he shuffled through the pictures, one in particular caught his attention. It was an image of a solitary man sitting on a bench overlooking the land; shimmering lights of green and gold hues were dancing in a geometric pattern in the night sky beyond him. The slump of the man's shoulders contrasted against the splendor the northern lights communicated. The man looked like he bore the weight of the world on his slumped shoulders. Or maybe, had been left behind and eagerly awaited the arrival of something out of the night sky?

Mr. Lanting checked which student had submitted this picture. George? *Didn't George tell me he only took pictures of animals?* It didn't matter. The picture made his mind wander, northern lights, alien beings, maybe some opening for a sci-fi movie, it all came pouring out of the image and into his consciousness. George had a gem here, but more importantly, didn't know it.

The following morning Mr. Lanting pulled George aside. "George, I must say your picture of the solitary man was intriguing. I thought you said you were only submitting pictures of the animals on your farm?"

George looked at the picture in Mr. Lanting's hand trying to remember it. Suddenly George remembered! He had been finishing up his evening chores one night and looked out of the barn to see his father in the distance. His father was just sitting on the bench staring out into night, looking defeated and tired. As George was taking the picture, there was a sudden burst of northern lights in the night sky. George hadn't thought much about it at the time and didn't realize that he had included the photo in his portfolio.

George replied, "I was taking pictures of the animals on the farm, but this sight was one I wanted to capture. I cannot recall a time when my father just sat looking dejected and in deep thought. He is always working. I guess it really didn't fit the assignment, I'm sorry Mr. Lanting."

"George, let me show you what makes this photo so good. The picture evokes an emotion that is palpable. It tells a story far beyond just a man sitting on a bench looking out into the night sky. The technical aspects of the picture are pretty good, but more importantly this picture has a voice, your voice George. That is what makes this photo stand out."

That day with Mr. Lanting was the day that George finally believed he really could be an artist and get away from the drudgery of the farm. He began submitting his pictures to various magazines and eventually had some published. George moved to the city, taking assignments wherever he could find them. Eventually he reached his goal, working on the staff of *National Geographic* just like his idol, Mr. Lanting.

After several years of living his dream, George returned home to help his father, who was in ill health. Even though he returned to the small town that he grew up in, it wasn't to be a farmer, but to teach photography. It was his turn to help a new generation of small-town kids learn how to see their world in a new light, just as his idol had all those years ago. ■

I realized the glow was coming from me. The light was in the center of my being!

Journey into Light
Chapter 1

BY RICK SHIGIO

The darkness was closing in on me. The thickness and insidiousness felt like a blanket that weighed a ton. The invasive void of light permeated into my spirit like black ink staining white linen. The walls of the toxic and stifling cave closed in as I walked. Abruptly, I was confronted with a wall blocking my path. The texture was rough and abrasive, a hard, thick, and impenetrable barrier made of ancient lava. I stood before it, befuddled. Pushing against the wall was futile, as it seemed to become even harder the more I tried.

Suddenly, the floor beneath me began to crumble and I began sinking into an abyss. There was nothing to grab, so I thrashed about, resisting the descent into who-knows-what. The more I struggled, the quicker I sank. Panic swept over me, and my only instinct was to flail about in desperation. I was overcome with a growing sense of dread; it was vain to grasp for any semblance of hope. Exhausted, I put my hands straight up and let myself fall.

Once I stopped struggling, the sinking slowed. Then I landed in a heap on the cold, smooth floor. But it was as solid as it could be. In the darkness, I felt around on my hands and knees. All I could feel was the floor and a pile of ashes. The remains of who I was and who I thought I was. Cold remnants of the past.

Forlorn and despondent, I curled into the fetal position and waited for the darkness to consume me. But the razing I expected never came. Eventually, my anxiety subsided and I was able to breathe again.

I lifted my head and noticed the faint glow of almost unperceivable light. Where was it was coming from? I stood and slowly walked around the space, looking for the source of that one glimmer. It was everywhere, but nowhere. I took a deep breath and closed my eyes. Then I opened them as wide as I could. What was that light? What was it emanating from?

I realized the glow was coming from me. The light was in the center of my being! The faint glow began to grow and there was even a trace of sparkle. I was still surrounded by blackness, but my inner light was starting to spread. An impulse told me to look up. I could see another faint glow above me. I began to feel a strange sense of calm, a lightness that I had never experienced. Something was lifting me up. I was floating and rising as my light began to illuminate my surroundings.

Moments later, I was facing the wall again. I had returned to where I had started. My small light revealed the rugged surface, the impenetrable wall. Yet as I turned around, I realized I had walked into a dead end of a cave. Pushing against the wall was futile, but by simply turning around, I found a way out.

As I emerged from the cave, I saw people walking by. Some had the same kind of small light emanating from inside of them, others did not. I was puzzled, as I had never seen this before. Or maybe I had just never noticed? One woman without a light from within was walking into the cave from which I had just escaped.

"Hey!" I yelled. "Don't go in there."

I ran back to the mouth of the cave, but she had already disappeared. The entrance was now just a flat wall. I touched what I thought was the entrance, but it was solid rock. I couldn't go in to stop her. I stood at that wall and my mind could not process what I had just seen.

"It's her path" a voice behind me announced.

It was Joan, my friend from the bank. I spun around and asked, "What?"

"It's her path, and only she could choose it or not."

I was confronted by my own confusion and exclaimed, "I don't understand!"

Joan graciously smiled, "It was your path, but not anymore. You did what you needed to do and went where you needed to go, so that door is now closed to you."

Joan was a lovely woman, there was great comfort in her smile and in her eyes. I noticed her wedding ring first, but then noticed that her light from within had a unique, iridescent quality.

"Come with me," she beckoned. "You must be hungry."

I felt like I was actually starving, so was easily persuaded.

Joan's husband, Ron greeted us at the door. "Welcome Rick." He extended his hand.

I perceived he too had that iridescent glow from within. I could not explain the unfamiliar yet reassuring feeling that came over me as I crossed the threshold of their home.

Their home was pleasingly decorated, and lively conversations were in progress as I entered the living room. About two dozen men and women were mingling, chatting and eating. The atmosphere was soothing, yet there was a subtle electric feeling as I walked across the floor. A sumptuous feast was set up on the dining room table with a wide assortment of enticing dishes artfully displayed. Joan handed me a plate, and began heaping servings of some of the dishes onto it. Yet only the ones that I found most enticing.

"How do you know what I want?"

"Just a lucky guess," she replied with a wink.

I had my suspicion that it was something more than just guessing.

A silver haired man reached out with an iced cup of punch. "I'm Herb. Here, you'll need a drink with all that food!" His pleasant demeanor and grand smile were engaging and personable.

"Thanks!" I replied. Herb flashed a wry grin and a wink.

A familiar hand touched my back. "Glad you finally made it." It was my old friend Dave, with a smirk on his face. "I hoped you would get here eventually. I've wanted you here for months."

"He's here now, and it is the perfect time," Ron interjected. "Eat up, we'll start soon."

The food had a calming effect, and I became more relaxed. Comfort food perhaps, but it was more the comforting environment.

Several folding chairs had been set up around the couch and love seat, and everyone was gathering into the small circle. From his chair to the side of the couch, Ron began to speak.

"Keep enjoying your food, and I will just start talking. You have all been invited, or have been drawn here because you are seeking something. Hopefully more than the great food, thanks to Joan, Janet, Carla and Herb."

There was a smattering of applause from those with their mouths full, including me.

Ron continued, "this opportunity for self-awareness and self-improvement may or may not be right for you, but it was right for many of us."

There were many knowing looks around the room.

"To be honest, it may not always be easy, because you will confront your greatest adversary. Someone who knows all about you, and may try very hard to undermine your progress. That person is you."

There were several befuddled looks, but I and several of the others realized exactly what Ron meant.

"Once you cross over, you will not be able to come back. But I expect you will not ever want to come back. That was my experience, and the experience of just about everyone else who has chosen this path."

Herb stood to speak. "I took this step five years ago, and I have not regretted it at all."

The light within him began to grow stronger and was almost flashing. "The positive changes I have made have impacted every facet of my life. My business is booming, my health is excellent, and all my relationships have improved by leaps and bounds."

His wife Bonnie took his hand and gave an approving smile.

"And tonight, my younger brother Edward has decided to finally get started."

Edward, sitting on the other side of Herb gave a wave and a smile. The light within him, although less noticeable, began to flash almost in sync with Herb.

Leslie, the affable and energetic blonde raised her hand. "What if I cross over, and don't like what I find?"

Joan smiled and replied, "what you will find is you, and you will always have the choice to determine what to do with what you find. There may be momentary discomfort with what you discover, but you will gain the awareness to make subsequent changes from where you are."

Joan's words had an obvious comforting effect and Leslie's smile grew broader.

Ron continued, "with that awareness, comes the vision to choose. Beyond this is all that you are, and all that you aren't. If this is not for you, thank you for being here. For those of you who choose in, you can follow me up the stairs. For those of you who are undecided, join me upstairs, and I can answer any remaining questions you might have."

I stood with my plate and started towards the kitchen. Herb reached out and took my plate and cup, and gestured towards the stairs.

"Go on up, I'll take care of this for you."

I saw the stairs and the door out. For a moment, I considered heading out the door, but something compelled me to take the stairs.

Upstairs, there was a long bench. There were several people sitting along bench, but the center was empty.

"Sit in the center," Dave suggested, even though my first instinct was to find a place on the side. "The center is where the most benefit can come. It's the Million Dollar seat," Dave continued, "yet most people avoid it."

Reluctantly, I took the center. Leslie sat next to me, and the bench was full.

Ron was standing to the side of the bench. "Now is the time of choice. Choose in, or choose out. We are here to encourage you, but only you can empower yourself to make this choice."

Before us appeared a pool of iridescent energy, swirling and constantly changing colors. Red, orange, yellow, green, blue, purple and violet. Repeating the same sequence over and over. The patterns were rhythmic yet random, another of the many paradoxes. Was it a barrier, or a portal? A wall or a door?

Ed stood up, and walked directly into the light, and disappeared. Leslie stood up, walked to the edge of the light and placed her hand into the light. A smile grew on her face, as she stepped forward and also disappeared. Gradually, one by one the others either stood and walked into the light or retreated back down the stairs.

I realized I was the last one, alone on that bench. I stared into the light that was foreboding and enticing at the same time. Walk through, or walk away? It boiled down to that simple choice. I remembered Ron's words: *Beyond this is all that you are, and all that you aren't.* I stood up and stepped to the edge. I reached out and felt a paradoxical warmth and coolness, as well as an electric vibration beginning to permeate through me. I took the step, and walked into the light. ■

It is better to die in the Plexus

than to live a coward,

Into the Plexus

BY CARMA SPENCE

Kirán looked out the observation deck portal at his destiny. The intricate network of stars, planets, and living space dust loomed bright and green not far off the port bow. This enigma of space had become the quest of choice for young nobles, and it was his turn to participate in the rite of passage.

The quest went like this: Enter the Plexus with not much more than a shuttlecraft. Survive for two days. Return ready and able to step into your adult role in life.

Most young nobles never returned. Only about five percent of those who entered the Plexus—noble or otherwise—ever returned. And of those, most of them were insane.

Kirán didn't want to go, but he had no choice. He was next in line to the throne and only the most dangerous quest would prove him worthy.

He could feel his body tremble ever so slightly, and his stomach felt heavy. His mouth was dry. He wanted to bolt and never return. But that would bring dishonor to his family.

"It is better to die in the Plexus than to live a coward," his father had told him just before Kirán boarded the ship that brought him here.

He heard the soft swoosh of the door opening. "Sire, it is time."

Kirán picked up his satchel containing all he was allowed to bring with him: two days' worth of food and water, a journal and pen, and a small light-dagger. He took one last look at the swirling green Plexus, then turned and followed the courtier into the passageway.

They walked quietly and solemnly toward the airlock where his shuttle was docked. Royal guard lined the walls, all at attention.

Kirán wondered if they were there for ceremony only…or to make sure he didn't back out of his duty. It was a fleeting thought, of no consequence. He knew what he had to do and had been raised for this act of courage all his young life.

They arrived at the portal. The courtier bowed low in deference to Kirán, then placed his hand upon the keypad, opening the airlock. Kirán saluted the courtier, then the royal guard, and then entered the shuttle pod, closing the airlock behind him.

The shuttle was compact, barely more than a life pod. There was a small cabinet for him to place his rucksack and a bench where he would sleep for the next two nights. The pilot's seat and console were at the front of the ship, a moderately sized view screen above them.

He hung his rucksack on the hook inside the cabinet and then took the pilot's seat. Flipping switches and checking readouts, he prepared to undock and fly into his future.

"You are clear for take-off," said a voice over the intercom.

"Thank you," Kirán replied. "I'll see you in two days." He hoped he sounded braver than he felt.

The shuttle jerked a bit as it undocked from the royal barge and then the spacecraft glided smoothly through space.

Two more clicks of a switch and he was racing toward the Plexus.

It loomed large in his fore portal. Soon he could see flashes of light skitter across the surface of the Plexus, like what he imagined sparks from neurons might look like. The inside of his shuttle was lit by an eerie green glow.

He took a deep, breath to calm himself and braced for entry.

Unlike other areas of space, the Plexus had a clear barrier demarcating where it began and normal space ended. He almost felt it as he entered. It was like a needle piercing the skin, a moment of resistance…

And then he was in.

Suddenly, all was quiet.

The blips and beeps that were the white noise of the shuttle had stopped. The hum of machinery working inside the walls and the console had ceased. It was like time itself had stopped.

And then he heard the voice.

The words appeared in his mind as if they were his own thoughts, but he could feel their alienness.

At least he assumed they were words, for he couldn't understand them. However, they had rhythm and pattern, so they must have formed a language.

A moment of this indecipherable chattering went on, and then he heard clearly and distinctly, "Kirán."

His heart raced. His face was cold. He barely got his response out from his parched mouth. "Yes?"

"You've been expected, young Kirán. Turn around to greet your guide."

He slowly turned around. Standing there was the most delicate and sublime woman he had ever seen. She was tall and had long, silver hair. Her eyes looked somewhat sad because they angled down on the outsides. Her gown covered her from neck to toe and glowed with a pale blue light. The cloth was diaphanous and opaque at the same time. Her skin was pale with touches of blue and green, like icebergs.

"We are Valo," she said. Her voice was silky smooth and had a slight echo as if she were speaking from inside a cavernous room. "We will be your guide through the Plexus. Fear not. You will not die this day."

Kirán had no idea how to reply. His mouth quivered into a smile, but he remained silent.

Valo moved to the bench and sat down. She was achingly graceful. He couldn't take his eyes off her. It was like he was in a trance.

"Come. Sit beside us," she said.

He rose from the pilot's seat, feeling like he was floating more than standing or walking, and took his place beside her, where he could see her face more clearly. It was somehow familiar, but he couldn't put his finger on it.

"The Plexus thought you would be more comfortable if we took on a familiar appearance," said Valo. "We took this face from your memories. They were old and fragile, so our resemblance may not be perfect."

That's when he realized whom she looked like.

When he was just a boy, he used to have an imaginary friend. Her name was Tará. He spent so much time with Tará that he had built an elaborate avatar for her in is mind. This avatar had a face that he would call forth when he felt particularly lonely. When he entered his teens, he left Tará behind. He had not thought of her until this moment.

Valo had Tará's face.

Kirán felt the blood rush away from his own face.

Valo tilted her head to one side in a quizzical expression. "Was the

Plexus mistaken?"

"Is this why all those men went mad?" Kirán thought. "Did their minds break when confronted with the imagination made real?" He took a breath. "I will not succumb."

"No, Kirán, you will not go mad," said Valo. "That is why we are here, to protect you from the inadvertent damage the Plexus wreaks on such fragile species as yourself. We are a gift."

"I don't understand," said Kirán.

"It matters not," she said. "You have no need to understand. Simply be. We will deliver you safely to the border in two days' time. Until then, we will guide you through the Plexus and show you wonderful things." ▪

...he lacked certain people

skills necessary to create a

flourishing business.

Bitter Brew

BY ANNA ZISS

The sky pulsated an unusual light through the old back window—otherworldly green brilliance punctuated with gold flecks like tiny stars dancing about the rising sun.

Jasper Glass Engel leaned across his kitchen sink and stared out the window. He found the colors intense, strange and oddly beautiful, ominous but inviting. How could the sky be green? He had been sober for a few years now, no drink or drugs, but perhaps this was some sort of flashback? Or maybe his imagination was especially strong this morning? Regardless of the reason, it was astonishing. He wondered how he could possibly reproduce the effects in a painting. Streaks of emerald green swirled, translucent, but dimensional, deep and seemingly infinite. He considered various possibilities: a layer of shiny, translucent epoxy over oil and gold leaf, maybe?

Jasper was a striking middle-aged man: a lithe, sinewy body, like that of a runner, but now a bit used and uneven; the face of a pre-Raphaelite angel marred by narrow, suspicious eyes; a halo of soft, black curls, accented with silvery streaks. As a younger man, his beauty played against an enigmatic personality, giving him an intriguing presence. An artist by nature and profession, he was prone to moodiness, self-absorption, and a love of denim overalls, worn for comfort a bit too big. He collected antique glass bottles—green, blue, and brown—that sat on his windowsill, reflecting today's strange light.

"What are you looking at, Jasper? More coffee before you get back to work?"

Jarred from his thoughts, Jasper turned abruptly, knocking a prized blue bottle into the sink. "I don't know how enjoyable that would be." He picked up the bottle, examining it for cracks or chips. "For either of us. I told you, I should always make the coffee," he grumbled. "Did you move my bottles? I like them like I leave them. Don't touch them." He gingerly placed the bottle back in a very specific place.

Wendy ignored his tone, got up from her spot at the kitchen table and filled another cup, pouring from the French press, stirring cream and sugar into the cloudy brew. "I tried a new kind. From that café. You know, with the barrels of different beans? I ground them myself. Here." She pointed to the small antique mill on the counter.

"I hate those cafés. So much attitude."

"It's a great place. I love going there. John and Elaine Overmeyer own it. Remember them? Elaine does those fabulous little botanical watercolors?" Wendy thought of the painting of violets Elaine had gifted to her, saying that the flowers reminded her of Wendy's eyes. Her eyes were still vibrant, but her long hair, once dark, was now white, matching her alabaster skin. White upon white, thin and melancholy, Wendy felt that she had faded over the years, paler and less visible with each passing year. One day soon, she was afraid, she would disappear altogether.

Wendy handed the cup to Jasper and leaned against the counter, watching her husband. He grunted, "The Overmeyers."

She could feel his jealousy. Elaine and John had thriving art careers as well as a café that doubled as their gallery. Jasper had been a mildly successful artist himself, but he lacked certain people skills necessary to create a flourishing business.

Jasper turned his attention back to the coffee. Wendy found it funny that his favorite drink was coffee, which he drank by the potful. As dark and bitter as he.

"This stuff is too acidy. It's hurting my stomach."

"Just sit down and relax." He snorted in reply but sat at the table and sipped his drink.

Jasper and Wendy had been married for several decades now. She had learned to ignore his moods, which in recent years turned to simple nastiness. Sometimes his ramblings amused her—his perspective was completely unique—but only when she forgot that there was sincerity behind his comments, not wit or irony. His words now cut with a constant malice that Wendy had come to overlook, too weary to argue.

"This coffee really is terrible. What did you say it was?"

"Seriously, Jasper." Wendy's voice rose uncharacteristically. "Do you need to complain about everything?"

"It tastes funny. Can you not even make coffee?"

"The coffee is fine," Wendy lowered her voice again. She was used to letting his insults roll over her. "It's Death Wish Coffee. The world's strongest coffee, they say."

"It tastes bad. Why aren't you drinking it?"

"I've had enough."

Wendy turned her back on her husband and turned her attention to cleaning up the kitchen. Opening a cabinet door, she put the mill back in its place. The cabinet was beautifully organized: a shelf of coffee and its accoutrements; a shelf of cups; a shelf of countless prescription bottles, grimy with charcoal dust or splatters of paint, as was much of their house. Some bottles bore her husband's name, others were unmarked, gotten from friends or bought on the street. So many bottles, so many "medicines," but none that seemed to work. Maybe they would work today.

"It tastes awful. Death Wish Coffee. Ha. Hipster coffee. It sounds overpriced, too."

"It was expensive. But I thought your last cup should be special."

Jasper drew in a sudden, long breath and wheezed. His face appeared green and hollow. One guttural groan and he slumped back in his chair.

Wendy looked over, scrunching up her face. "Oh, my goodness. It must've been a suicide."

Rising, she walked to her windowsill, scooped up the bottles and threw them in the trash. "That coffee? It's called Best Morning Ever." She smiled as she walked past the old back window. She had never seen a sky so clear and blue. ■

Starchez

Photo courtesy of Starrchez. © 2019 Canon Vision Media

Los Angeles born and raised, Starr Canon a.k.a. Starrchez has been in the photography industry for over seven years.

She began her career in music production, song writing and recording engineering. She then began to experiment with photography and videography, developing a much sought after colorful and expressive style of visual art. Canon Vision Media was born to accommodate the new demands.

Armed with an industry background, thick skin and a deep love and respect for music, art, fashion, culture and film, Starrchez has a natural gift for working with artists, performers, DJ's and models. Helping them unleash their inner talents in a safe, creative, and laid-back environment is her specialty.

In 2019, Starrchez added screenplay writing, cinematography and film-making to her arsenal. *Hunter*, her first short film was recently completed and submitted to film festivals worldwide. ■

Members of the Rough Writers Toastmasters Club who contributed stories to this volume:

Susan Cameron.. *charter member*

Cynthia Gellis.. *member since 2019*

Christopher Gildemeister .... *charter member*

Terrell Harrison .... *charter member*

Benjamin Horak .... *member since 2019*

Cary Kellems .... *member since 2018*

James Kinstle... *member since 2018*

David Kitchen... *charter member*

Lola! Love .... *member since 2018*

Lydia Martinez .... *charter member*

Rick Shig*io*... *member since 2018*

Carma Spence.. *charter member*

Anna Ziss .... *member since 2019*

ROUGH WRITERS

TOASTMASTERS CLUB

Where speakers become writers

writers become speakers.

MONDAYS 7 – 8:15 PM

FIRE STATION #8
5373 EAST 2ND STREET
LONG BEACH, CA 90803

ROUGHWRITERS.TOASTMASTERSCLUBS.ORG